M000031971

Home Run

by Di Pert
illustrated by Anna Godwin

SCHOOL PUBLISHERS

Ming was at a new school.

"Come with us," said Sam.

"You can pass the ball to me, Ming."

Ming had strong arms.
She held the ball over her head.
She passed it by Sam.

"Can you try and toss the ball
in the net?" asked Sam.
Ming jumped with the ball.
She tried hard, but the ball went
way up past the net.

4

Ming looked sadly down at her feet.

"It's no good," she said.

"I just can't get the ball in the net."

Sam got a bat and a ball and
handed them to Ming.
"Use your arms, Ming!" said Sam.

Ming swung the bat hard.

"You are good at this," said
Ming's new friend, Sam.
"You hit a home run every time!"